The Golden Acorn

Janice V. Edwards

An imprint of Mearas House Publishing

ISBN-13: 978-0-9882390-1-2

At Home

Acorn looked up admiringly at his father Quicksilver as he ran about the branches overhead. It was a bright morning in May with the trees breaking out with new leaves. Every now and then Quicksilver would leap several yards from one tree to another, and Acorn would catch his breath.

"I wish I could do that," he thought. Acorn was a squirrel who had just been born that spring and he was too young yet to take such long flying leaps.

Wham! Something hit him from behind, and he went sprawling. It was his brother Oakleaf ready for another tussle and chase. Up the nearest tree they went as fast as a wink one after the other.

But they were interrupted by their sister Poppy calling from the hollow in the hickory tree to come for breakfast. Their home was up high with cupboards around the walls and a stair on one side leading up to the bedrooms or down to the storage rooms. They all sat around the table eating hickory nut porridge and chattering the way squirrels do. Quicksilver said, "I think I'll go visit Hoot the owl and get some news."

"Can I come? Can I come?" all the little squirrels cried.

"Not today. It's a long way, and you would be tired out before we were halfway. Tomorrow I'll take you to visit your cousin Whippersnapper instead".

"Hurray!" they said – all except Acorn who imagined himself jumping lightly from tree to tree behind his father.

"Acorn, Oakleaf, and Poppy, you all help your mother today while I'm gone and don't get into any trouble." said Quicksilver.

"Don't worry about us," said Sesame, their mother. We have lots of spring cleaning to do, and I have a job for everyone."

"Well, I'll be off," said Quicksilver. And he scampered out and was gone in a flash.

Poppy began doing the breakfast dishes and Oakleaf straightened the storerooms downstairs while Acorn dragged his feet bemoaning his fate. He was supposed to be taking out the hickory shells leftover from breakfast. He felt like life was passing him by.

"If you do your work well, you all can go out to play when you're finished," coaxed Sesame, hoping to lift Acorn's spirits. Even that didn't help. But soon after, a sparkle arose in his eye, and his little feet danced. He had an idea!

He wanted to do something special and exciting. There was one thing he had always wanted to do and today was the perfect day for it. Among the animals there was a story about a tree with golden nuts in the depths of the Whispering Wood. If anyone brought home a nut from this tree, he would never need to gather food again and would always have plenty. It's true that his father Quicksilver had never been too pleased with the story and showed no interest in seeking this wonderful prize, but Acorn couldn't understand that. There was a problem though-The Whispering Wood was known as a dark mysterious place full of unknown creatures and dangers. That was hard to imagine because where Acorn now stood the sun was warm on his back, the grass was green under the flickering shadows from the trees, a soft breeze was tussling his fur, and there was a lovely smell of growing things in the air

"Nothing could go wrong today," he thought.

As soon as Acorn was finished with his work, he cornered Oakleaf in a quiet spot where no one could hear them. "I'm going to the Whispering Wood to find the Golden Acorn. If you promise to do as I say, I'll let you come". Acorn really didn't want to go alone, and he wisely guessed Oakleaf would be a more willing partner if he appeared to be 'letting' him come rather than begging him.

"You know we're not supposed to go near there, Acorn. It's spooky!" answered Oakleaf.

"Oh, that's for babies!" said Acorn. "We're much bigger and stronger now, and I'm not afraid." He looked at Oakleaf accusingly.

"I'm not afraid either," said Oakleaf quickly. "When do we start?"

The Journey

So off they went without a backward glance. Sometimes they ran through the branches and sometimes along the ground. Poppy saw them leave from their hollow and called out to them, but they didn't hear her. Little James Jay saw them scampering along the branches near him and asked, "Where are you going? Can I come too?"

"No, No," said Acorn. "You can't fly well enough yet. We're going to find the Golden Oak Tree. But don't tell anyone! It's a secret."

When they only had a short way to go to the wood, they took to the ground as a little meadow lay ahead of them. A few of their young rabbit friends were playing on the edge of the meadow.

"Where are you going?" asked Daisy. "Have you come to play with us?"

"Not today," said Acorn. "We're on a journey."

"What kind of a journey?" asked Bigfoot.

"A secret journey, so you mustn't tell anyone. We're going to find the Golden Oak Tree!"

"Ooooooh!" they chorused.

"Let me come!" said Bigfoot.

"No, you would have trouble keeping up," said Acorn. "We will be travelling through the trees too." Without another thought for their friend, Acorn and Oakleaf scurried off.

As they approached the wood, they saw a wide stream coursing its way along the edge. At first they could see no way across, but Oakleaf noticed a tall tree with branches nearly stretching to the branches of the trees on the other side.

"I'm sure we can leap that far," said Acorn, with a not so confident look in his eye. They climbed the tree, and Acorn crept slowly out to the end of the branch as it wavered in the wind. It looked awfully far down to the swift stream below and much further to the waiting branch on the other side than it had from the ground.

He decided if he was to make it across, he would have to run for it. So he went back along the branch, took a deep breath and started again as fast as he could go. Nimbly, he hopped from the end of the branch across the gap to the tree on the other side, catching a branch and dangling for a moment before pulling himself up safely. Meanwhile, Oakleaf had been watching speechless from the other side.

"Acorn, I don't think I can do it," he cried.

"Oh, it wasn't so bad," said Acorn with a pang of guilt, knowing it really was pretty bad. But he so wanted to go on!

"You can do it!" he called.

Oakleaf began running and then leapt. His paw brushed the leaves on the other side, but he missed and fell into the moving stream below!

"Oakleaf, I'm coming!" yelled Acorn. He scrambled down the tree and ran along the edge calling to Oakleaf, "I'm coming! Don't drown!" Oakleaf was struggling to stay above water, and Acorn didn't know how to help him. He prayed, "Dear God, Please forgive me for bringing him into this danger!"

As if in answer to his prayer, Oakleaf reached out for a branch that was caught against the shore. He climbed up on it and gradually made his way to the bank.

Acorn was there waiting for him. "Oakleaf, I'm so glad you're all right! Lay down here in the sun and I'll go find something for you to eat."

He went a short way into wood which was oppressive and dark even along the edge. He saw some walnuts here and there on the ground a few yards ahead, but it took all his courage to go gather them. He heard strange rustlings even though there was no wind, and the air seemed thick, and moss hung from the trees. He felt he couldn't see clearly, He darted forward and stuffed some of the nuts into his cheeks and ran back the way he had come. For a moment, he panicked as he felt something soft and sticky brushing his fur, but it was only a spider web. He hurried back to Oakleaf who has beginning to feel better. They sat in the grass and ate their nuts, slowly recovering from their excitement.

It was peaceful in the grass, and Oakleaf was drying out. Their snack gave them courage, but they were both tired, and they unwillingly dozed off. Acorn woke with a start several hours later. The shadow of the trees had fallen across them and the chill woke him up. But it was only mid-afternoon, and Acorn forgot his concern for Oakleaf and urged him on.

"Wake up! We still have time to find the tree!" Oakleaf woke up cheerful and ready as always to follow Acorn's suggestion.

"Do you think we can really find it?" he asked. "It looks like such a big place."

"Do you remember the poem we heard from Dusty Owl? He heard it from his father. It goes:

> The Golden Tree with the Golden Fruit
> Lies deep within the Whispering Wood.
> The Silver Stream may lead you there,
> But none will find it unless he dare
> The dangers that therein lay,
> And his heart show him the Way.

This couldn't be the Silver Stream because it doesn't lead into the wood, but maybe it branches off from it," said Acorn.

Just then they heard a rustling from the woods behind them. Automatically they both scurried up the nearest tree. A large porcupine lumbered out of the woods. He didn't look very threatening so Acorn whispered to Oakleaf, "Maybe we should ask him where the stream is." So he called down.

"Excuse me, Mr. Porcupine, but do you know if the Silver stream branches off this river anywhere nearby?"

"Hmm, hmm," said the porcupine. "Well, I just don't know. This here river is called The Winding Way, but I've never heard of the Silver Stream...but there is a little creek down river a short way, but I've never heard it called anything but the Old Creek. I wouldn't go that way if I were you. It's not safe!" And he lumbered off upstream.

"We'll have to try it," said Oakleaf. So they hopped from branch to branch still staying near the edge of the Winding Way.

Soon they saw a sparkling brook join the river.

"This must be it!" they cried. On they went happily frisking along. But soon the darkness of the wood began closing in, and the feeling in the air wasn't so nice. They kept on, and it got darker and darker even though it was still afternoon. The silence seemed to cry out at them. There were no sounds of birds, only the rustle of trees.

All of a sudden, they heard a loud commotion down on the ground. Something was running towards them through the leaves that carpeted the forest floor. A small raccoon came into sight and ran quickly up the very tree in which they sat.

Close behind the raccoon was a huge slavering grey wolf with long teeth and claws. His jaws snapped closing inches behind the raccoon. He growled and barked and jumped, but he couldn't get up the tree.

"I'll get you somehow!" he hissed.

The squirrels felt sorry for the raccoon and told him who they were and where they were going.

"My name is Clever," he panted. "But I don't think it was so clever of me to let myself be spotted by this wolf!"

"Maybe we can escape him by going from branch to branch. In this light if we're quiet he won't even know we're gone," said Acorn. "If you were full grown, I'm not sure we could make it because you would be too heavy."

"Let's try it," said Clever. "Thank you for your help." In that way they quietly escaped the wolf.

It was difficult for the raccoon in the trees, so as soon as they were safe from the wolf, he wanted to go back to the ground to travel.

"I may be able to help you," Clever said. "I've done some exploring in these woods, and there is one spot I'm thinking that tree might be. I haven't seen it though. Inside the wood a bit farther is a high hedge made of briars in a big circle. No one knows what is inside because the hedge is so thick and thorny."

"Let's try it," said Acorn.

"We'd better hurry," said Oakleaf. "It's getting late."

They travelled awhile longer, and then Clever turned down an overgrown pathway leading towards the thorny barrier that they hoped guarded the tree. The two squirrels joined Clever on the ground and stared at the high hedge in front of them. Big thorns and little thorns joined to heavy branches which were thickly entwined forming a wall that no light could pass through.

"How shall we get through?" said Oakleaf. "We can't give up now!"

"We'll have to use our heads to solve this problem," said Acorn. They all walked around the hedge looking high and low for any possible gaps.

At last Clever said, "The only way I see would be for one of you to climb to the top of that tree and swing down over the thicket holding onto a long strand of that moss hanging from the tree. But I don't know how you could come back!"

"I'll try it," said Acorn quickly, heedless of the problem concerning his return trip.

"You could climb back up the moss that you use to get in, but you would probably be dragged over the thorns on the way up," said Clever.

"That's a small price to pay," called Acorn as he climbed the tree. He grabbed a long piece of moss and pulled it back to get a good swing over the top of the thicket.

"Be careful!" said Oakleaf.

Whoosh! Acorn flew over the edge of the thorns dangling from the trailing moss. He let go and tumbled to the ground inside the enclosure. For a moment he was stunned by his fall, but hadn't hurt himself, so he slowly got up and looked around.

The glade was very different from the surrounding forest. The sun was just setting behind the treetops. It was warm and full of light. There were small fruit trees and a spring was gurgling a little way off. It was so peaceful he felt he could have sat there in the grass for ages. But his friends were calling to him.

"Are you all right, Acorn?"

"I'm fine," he called back. "I'm going to look for the tree."

He got up and walked toward the spring. It looked so fresh and cool that he stopped to take a drink. It tasted wonderful and he was refreshed. Beyond the pool he caught a glimpse of something flashing in the light of the setting sun. "That must be it," he thought. And he ran towards it, his heart beating wildly.

It was a beautiful tree, large with widespread branches. The leaves were green with flashing under sides that looked like gold dust. Hints of gold shone from the bark here and there. From below, he couldn't see any golden acorns but it was a tall tree. He thought he'd better have a closer look by climbing it, but it seemed wrong to touch such an awe-inspiring creation. "Dear God," he prayed, "Please help me to find a golden acorn to take home to my family."

He took courage and touched the base of the tree. Nothing happened so he began climbing. As he reached the branches, he saw clusters of little golden acorns nestled under the leaves. He ran down one of the branches and reached for a little nut. It was a perfect acorn and yet made of pure gold. It even felt heavy. Acorn stored it in his cheek and turned to go back down, but stopped.

"Why not take more? There are plenty here," he thought. Although he lifted his paw, something within held him back. Something was telling him that it was greedy to take more and it would turn a good thing into an evil one.

So instead he turned and hurried down the tree. There was no time to lose because it was getting dark. He ran back to the place where he had dropped to the ground. He saw the moss dangling over the thorny wall that separated him from his friends. It looked like it would be very painful to climb out that way, but he steeled himself and called to his friends, "I've got it. I'm coming!"

But as he began his ascent, he suddenly found himself standing outside the thorny hedge.

"Hurray!" he thought. "This *is* a mysterious place!" But his joy quickly turned to worry when he looked around and couldn't see Clever and Oakleaf anywhere. Although he called their names he heard no answer. The forest was now still and growing dark. Acorn knew they wouldn't have deserted him and realized something unusual must have happened!

Acorn looked all over the ground for clues. All he could see in the fading light was a mark on the leafy forest floor as if something had been dragged along the ground, parting the leaves. He followed the trail as best he could for what seemed like forever. He was losing hope, and feeling guilty that he hadn't taken good care of his little brother. "Dear God, Forgive me again for only thinking of myself." he cried. The tears rolled down his furry cheeks. He came to a clearing with a small ramshackle house in the center. He slowly and warily scampered up to the house but saw no sign of life.

Around back he heard someone call his name.

"Acorn, Acorn, we're over here." Acorn eagerly ran toward the sound of Oakleaf's voice. He found the two friends locked in a cage with a heavy padlock on the door.

"Oakleaf, Clever, I'm so glad to see you, but what happened, why are you in a cage?"

"Shhh, the evil magician will be back any minute. We've got to get out of here. He's planning to feed us to his pet lion. If you could pull the pins from the hinges, the door would come open. I think I could do it but I can't reach them." Acorn tried and tried, but his paws and teeth weren't strong enough.

"Oh, what shall we do?" said Acorn.

"Let's ask God to help us," said Oakleaf. "He saved me from the water and he can save us from the magician too."

"How can God help us?" asked Clever doubtfully. "I can't see Him."

"My dad says it's the things we can't see that are the most important, like Love and God," said Oakleaf.

"Whooosssssssshhh" a loud swooping noise came near and Acorn ran away hiding in a bush just as a large owl landed on the cage. Another one landed immediately after. It was Hoot the owl and his friend Fiddle-dust.

"We've found you at last!" they said. Acorn came tumbling out just in time to see his father Quicksilver arrive.

"I'm glad to see you, Dad!" he cried.

"I'm glad to see you too, but we've no time to talk now." The owls and Quicksilver began working on the cage hinges. Soon they had the door off and Clever and Oakleaf were free.

"Let's get back as quickly as we can now," said Quicksilver. The owls led the way back and by morning they were all back at their own homes.

Home Again

After a big meal and a long sleep, Oakleaf and Acorn were ready to have a talk with Quicksilver about their long journey. Acorn and Oakleaf apologized for going off on a forbidden trip.

"Thank you for apologizing," said Quicksilver, "I think it would be best for you two to do some extra work around the house to show that you're sorry. But at the same time I want to say how pleased I am at the courage you showed. I know you felt you were providing for our family by bringing back the golden acorn.

"You may wonder why I never went to look for it myself. I feel that God made our family strong and healthy and has given us abundant food in the woods. Gathering nuts and seeds each year is the work God gives us squirrels, and it's a good thing for us to work for a living. To have a golden acorn is not necessary for us and could even be bad for us because we would become idle."

"But Dad," Acorn broke in, feeling badly that all his efforts had gone towards acquiring something so little needed.

"Let me finish," said Quicksilver. "There are others that could benefit from this golden acorn. Can you think of any way you could put it to good use?"

Acorn looked at his feet and thought. He knew what his father meant. He could give it away. It was difficult to lose his hard-won golden treasure, but he could see that it was more loving to share it with someone who needed it more than he did.

"How about giving it to Aunt Primrose?" said Acorn. "Ever since Uncle died she has struggled to get enough food for all her babies."

"That's a very good idea, Acorn," said Quicksilver. "What do you say, Oakleaf?"

"Yes let's. Let's do it right away." Down the tree they scrambled and off to Aunt Primrose's house. When Aunt Primrose received the golden acorn she was so happy that she cried. She kissed both of the squirrel boys and thanked them.

Acorn and Oakleaf scampered off happily chasing and tumbling all over each other. Acorn was surprised that he didn't feel sad. He not only didn't feel sad, he was happy! He'd had a wonderful adventure, and he'd helped his aunt so that she and her family would never be hungry again. To work every day in serving family, neighbors, and God, isn't that real joy after all!

The End

About the Author

Janice V. Edwards lives with her husband David in the countryside near Charlottesville, Virginia. They have three grown children and eight grandchildren who reside in Virginia and Switzerland. Janice is a watercolor artist who loves to paint animals and gardens, and she also surrounds herself with animals and gardens.

She originally wrote and illustrated "The Golden Acorn" in 1987, but the manuscript and paintings were eventually lost.

More than 30 years later, in 2018, Janice suffered a brain aneurysm and nearly died. Today she is still recovering, and is now unable to paint or garden as she did before, and even simply communicating is difficult.

It was also in 2018, following her major health emergency, that Janice's husband David remembered "The Golden Acorn" and began searching for it. Two years later he discovered the little treasure intact in a storage box. He decided to publish the book as a gift for the friends and family who have supported them through their trial.

Janice and David are grateful for all the help and prayers they have received, and are especially grateful to God for His mercy in preserving Janice's life and for the ongoing recovery and healing of her mind and body.

They hope friends and family will enjoy this book, and perhaps new readers too, who may also become their friends.